Playing in the Snow

Colleen Adams

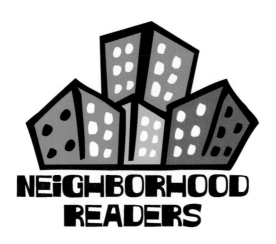

NEiGHBORHOOD READERS

Rosen Classroom Books & Materials™

New York

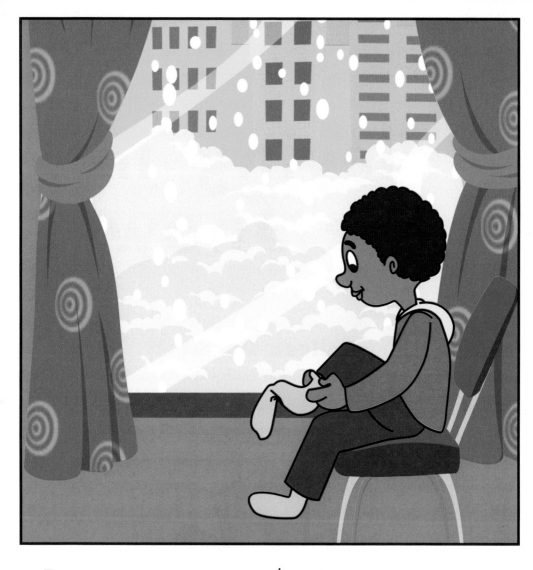

I put on my socks.

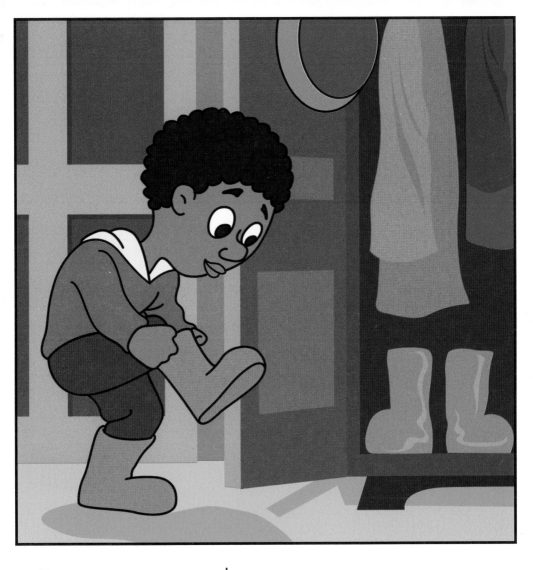

I put on my boots.

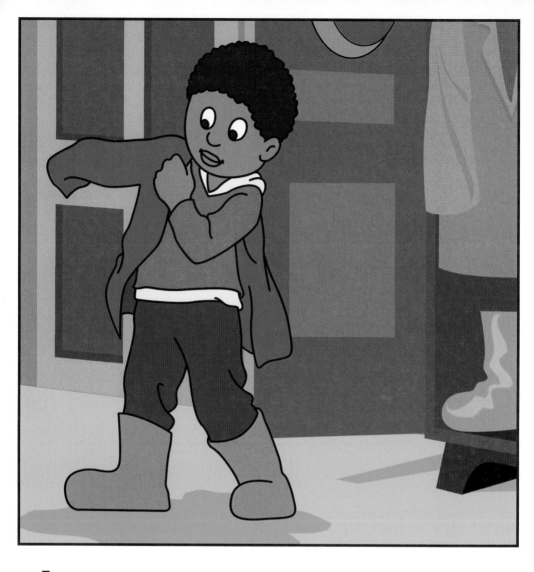

I put on my coat.

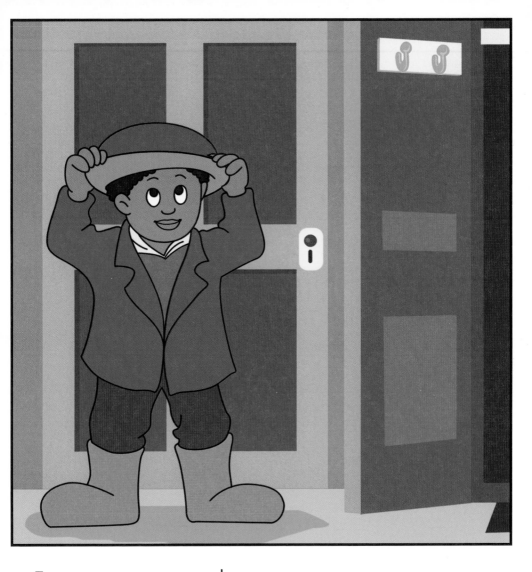

I put on my hat.

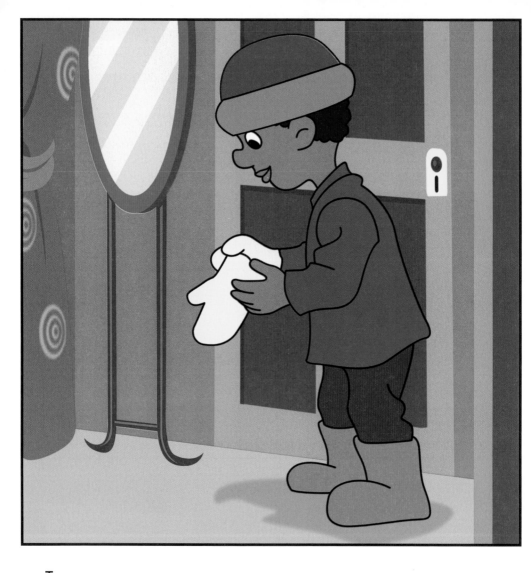

I put on my mittens.

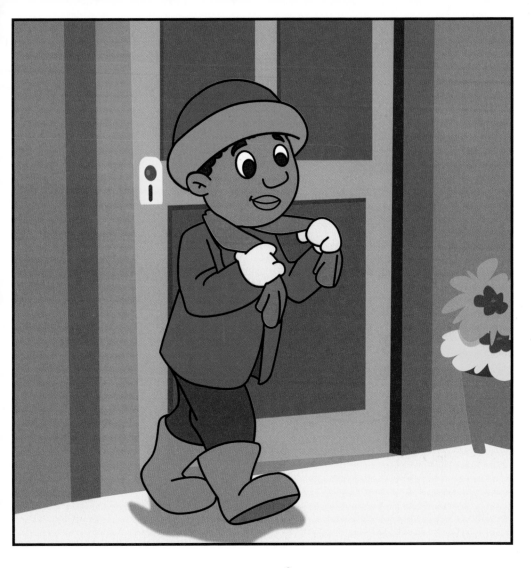

I put on my scarf.

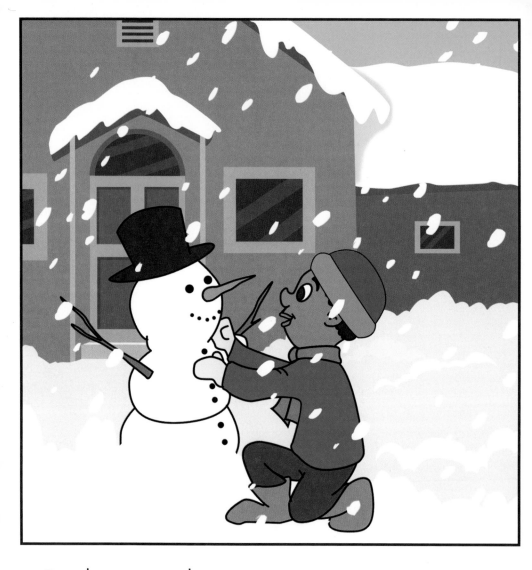

I play in the snow.